EVERYTHING REALLY
IMPORTANT HAPPENS

WHEN WE'RE BLINKING

Some Thoughts for my friends

To Share With Your friends

by mari stein

Words and drawings by Mari stein
copyright © 1974, 1977 by Mari stein
all rights reserved
first edition: 1974
second edition: november 1977
published by Quarterdeck Press
Box 134, Pacific Palisades
California 90272

YOU CAN HAVE HALF MY OREO
THE GOOD SIDE WITH THE GOO

THERE ARE REALLY NO SECRETS
ONLY UNDISCUSSED THINGS

WE CAN FIND A WAY

first
Class
Stamp
Here

IT'S NOT SO MUCH MY FAILURES
THAT BOTHER ME
BUT OTHER PEOPLES' SUCCESSES

first
Class
Stamp
Here

I'M TRYING TO MAKE ME SMILE
WHILE YOU'RE AWAY

MESSAGE

I WAS JUST A WEED
WHEN I MET YOU

MESSAGE

first
Class
Stamp
Here

IN LOVE THERE'S ROOM
FOR ALL OF US
AND THE SUN AND THE MOON
AND THE STARS
TO SNUGGLE IN SOON

PLEASE LISTEN TO WHAT I MEAN

first
Class
Stamp
Here

THIS IS THE DAWNING OF
THE AGE OF AQUARIUMS

YOU SAY YOU LOVE ME MORE
WHEN I'M PLAIN

BUT YOU WANT ME MORE
WHEN I'M PRETTY

MESSAGE

first
Class
Stamp
Here

I GAVE AN OAK A POKE

YOU CAN'T QUITE FORGET YOU MISS SOMEONE
EVEN THOUGH YOU CAN'T QUITE REMEMBER

MESSAGE

I'VE GOT THE MASHED POTATOES AND GRAVY BLUES

MESSAGE

I'M TIRED OF FEELING SORRY
FOR THREE LEGGED DOGS
WHO SADDEN MY DAY
THEN GO MERRILY ON THEIR WAY

I HAVEN'T GOT TIME FOR LOVE OR HATE
TALKING OR TOUCHING,
LOOKING OR SEEING, HEARING OR FEELING -
I'M JUST GOING TO SIT HERE AND WAIT
FOR SOMETHING IMPORTANT TO HAPPEN

MESSAGE

I FEEL LIKE THE SECOND PERSON
THE ONE FORGOTTEN ON THE SINKING SHIP
WHILE ALL THE RIGHT PEOPLE
ARE BUSY GETTING SAVED

MESSAGE

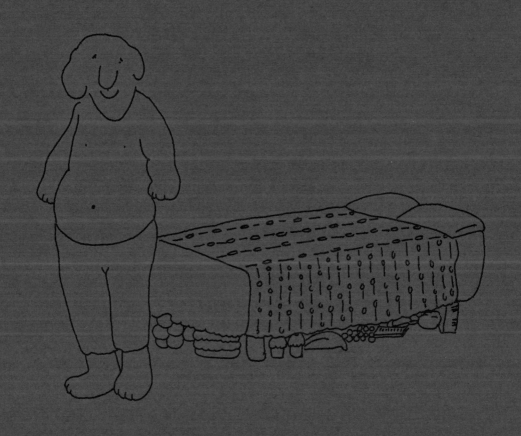

DIET QUIETLY

MESSAGE

First
Class
Stamp
Here

MESSAGE

ALL I ASK FOR IS A LITTLE MAGIC IN MY LIFE
FOR THAT SPOTTED DOG TO SAY HELLO BACK
WHEN I PASS HIM ON THE STREET CORNER
AND TO SEE AN ELEPHANT SMILE
ON MY WAY HOME

THERE'S NO SUBSTITUTE FOR QUANTITY

first
Class
Stamp
Here

GREY MORNINGS GIVE THE HEAVENS
TIME TO THINK

I AM STARING AT MY TYPEWRITER
IT IS STARING BACK AT ME
IT SAYS OLIVETTI UNDERWOOD
I DON'T SAY ANYTHING

I MUST BE GETTING BETTER —
I DON'T THINK ABOUT KILLING MYSELF ANYMORE
I THINK ABOUT KILLING EVERYBODY ELSE . . .

I THINK PERHAPS I JUST SHOULD HAVE GIVEN YOU ONE PERFECT ROSE PETAL

MESSAGE

I'D BE HAPPY IF I COULD JUST SPEND THE REST
OF MY LIFE TURNING OVER TURTLES

MESSAGE

WHERE'S YOUR MOMMY WHEN YOU NEED HER
AND YOU'RE ALL GROWN UP

MESSAGE

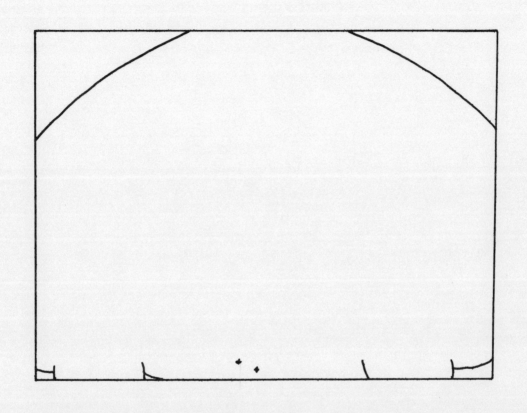

MAYBE WE'RE ALL JUST ANTS CRAWLING UP
THE SIDE OF A GIANT HIPPOPOTAMUS
FOR A HUNDRED YEARS

HICCUPS ARE FOR LITTLE KIDS

WHY DO THEY CALL IT YOUR LAST DYING BREATH
WHEN IT'S YOUR LAST LIVING BREATH

CAN YOU REMEMBER: PARTY LINES
AND SEN SEN AND COFFEE CANS
YOU OPENED WITH KEYS
THAT YOU CUT YOURSELF ON...

AND CHASING CATS
AND BITING MAILMEN
AND CHEWING BONES
AND BARKING AT....

MESSAGE

YOU'RE NOT ALONE
THE GUILTIES ARE ALWAYS LURKING

first
Class
Stamp
Here

DO YOU ONLY WANT ME
SO NO ONE ELSE WILL HAVE ME...

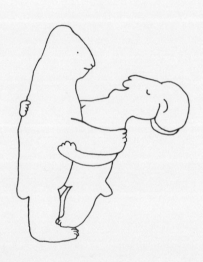

NO WORDS ARE ACCURATE ENOUGH...
THAT IS... WORDS ARE NOT ACCURATE ENOUGH...
I MEAN NO WORDS AREN'T EITHER...
SEE WHAT I MEAN?

LIFE AIN'T ALL JUST CARROTS AND CLOVER YOU KNOW

MESSAGE

I'M JUST SITTING HERE
WAITING FOR NATURE TO DO HER THING

SOMETIMES I JUST WALK AROUND
LOOKING FOR NEW SHAPES TO LOVE
WHILE I'M THERE I SEE PEOPLE
LOOKING FOR NEW LOVES TO SHAPE

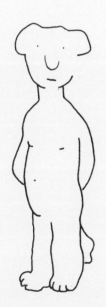

OWW - I GOT MY SPLINTER
IN A TOE...

MESSAGE

first
Class
Stamp
Here

A SONG IS WHAT YOUR HEART GIVES YOU
TO KEEP YOU FROM GOING CRAZY

PLEASE DONT MAKE ME LAUGH
CAN'T YOU SEE THAT I'M BUSY
CONCENTRATING ON MY PROBLEMS

MESSAGE

THERE'S EITHER TOO MUCH TO SAY

OR NOT ENOUGH

MESSAGE

GO AHEAD THINK YOURSELF INTO OBLIVION

MESSAGE

LISTENING IS THE ART OF GETTING THE OTHER
PERSON TO GET WHAT HE HAS TO SAY
OVER WITH AS FAST AS YOU CAN
SO YOU CAN RELAX AND SAY YOURS

BLAME IT ON ME

FEELING SORRY FOR YOURSELF
DOESN'T SERVE ANY USEFUL PURPOSE
IT'S JUST THAT WHEN YOU FEEL THAT BAD
THERE'S NOTHING BETTER TO DO

I DON'T EVEN HAVE A WISH

I'M YOURS

First Class Stamp Here

YOU BELONG TO BE WITH ME

I BELONG TO BE WITH YOU

MESSAGE

LET US TAKE SOME JOY
IN THE FUTILITY OF IT ALL

MESSAGE

I REALLY SHOULDN'T SAY THIS BUT...
I DON'T WANT TO HURT YOUR FEELINGS BUT...

FIND MORE HUGS

MESSAGE

THE COW JUST SAT AND SAT
AND DIDN'T THINK ONCE ABOUT THE MOON

MESSAGE

SO MUCH HATE WE STORE
FROM SO LONG AGO
AND SAVE IT UP TO WASTE
ON THE WRONG PERSON

I'M STUCK WITH THE GUILT
OF YOUR GENERATION
AND THE LETHARGY
OF MINE

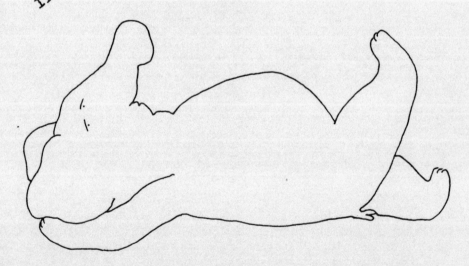

Other Books By Mari Stein

So You're Going To Have Puppies

VD The Love Epidemic

The Contraception Book

MESSAGE